How the Stars Fell into the Sky

A Navajo Legend

Jerrie Oughton   Illustrated by Lisa Desimini

Houghton Mifflin Company   Boston   1992

Library of Congress Cataloging-in-Publication Data

Oughton, Jerrie.
  How the stars fell into the sky : a Navajo legend / Jerrie Oughton ;
illustrated by Lisa Desimini.
      p.   cm.
  Summary: A retelling of the Navajo legend that explains the
patterns of the stars in the sky.
  ISBN 0-395-58798-0
  1. Navajo Indians—Legends.   [1. Navajo Indians—Legends.
2. Indians of North America—Southwest, New—Legends.]
I. Desimini, Lisa, ill.   II. Title.
E99.N3088   1992   91-17274
398.2'089972—dc20   CIP
                          AC

Text copyright © 1992 by Jerrie Oughton
Illustrations copyright © 1992 by Lisa Desimini

Printed in the United States of America

HOR   10 9 8 7 6 5 4 3 2 1

This book is dedicated to my family

Paul
Cher and Dale and Caroline and Kyle
Lisa and Bob
Shannon and Ross
Sean
Preston

and to a very special teacher
who never let me let go the dream
Mrs. Peacock

—J.O.

For Matthew, Anthony, and Nina Marie Puma

—L.D.

This is a retelling of a legend told
to the Navajo Indians by Hosteen Klah,
their great medicine man,
at the turn of the twentieth century.
It is part of the mythology that details the
mysteries of Earth in the beginning.

When the pulse of the first day carried it to the rim of night, First Woman said to First Man, "The people need to know the laws. To help them, we must write the laws for all to see."

"Write them in the sand," he told her.
"But the wind will blow them away," she answered.

"Write them on the water then," he said and turned to go, having more important matters on his mind.

"But they will disappear the moment I write them on the water," First Woman called out.

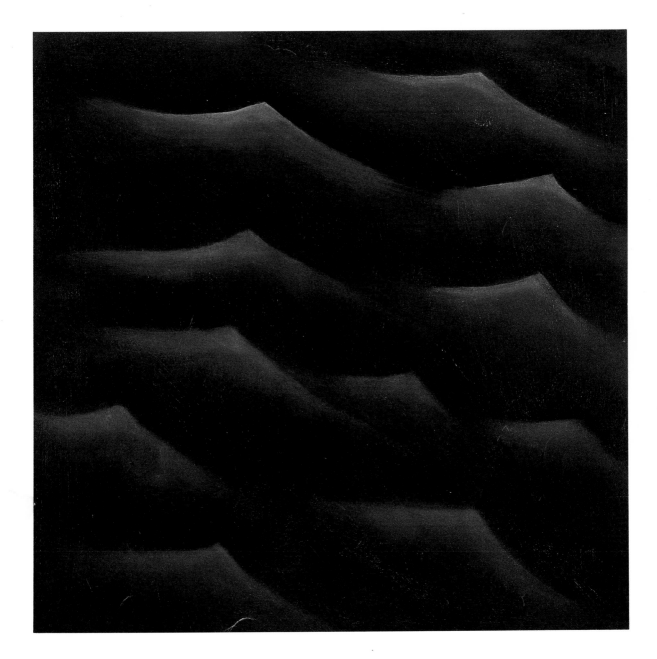

First Man turned back impatiently and looked at her squatting there on the rim of night, a blanket of stars at her feet.

"Why don't you write them in the sky?" he said.
"Take your jewels there and write them in the sky."

And so she began, slowly, first one and then the
next, placing her jewels across the dome of night,
carefully designing her pattern so all could read it.

But First Woman was not alone. Behind a low
tree Coyote crouched, watching her as she crafted
her careful mosaic on the blackberry cloth of night.
He crept closer.

"What are you doing?" he called to her in a voice that sounded like the whine of an arrow whistling in the wind. "Why are you tacking up the night sky with your jewels?"

"Oh," she answered, deliberately shifting a star, "I am writing the laws so all the people can read them. There will be no confusion if we can always see the laws."

Her hands glowed from the warmth of the stars she was touching, and she smiled as she toiled.

"May I help?" Coyote asked.

First Woman nodded. "Begin here," she said and handed him a star.

Coyote hung the star and stepped back to look.
He hung another, and another. But for each star he
hung, First Woman's blanket held a hundred
thousand more.

"This is slow work," he grumbled.

"Writing the laws could take many moons," she said and began humming to herself.

"Can't we find a faster way and be done?" Coyote asked.

"Why finish?" she answered. "What is there to do next that is half so important as writing the laws?"

"The people will see these laws before they enter their hogans at night."

"The young mother will sing of them to her child."

"The lonely warrior, crouching in an unknown country, will look up and warm himself by them."

"Writing the laws may be what I do each night for the rest of my life."
But Coyote lacked First Woman's patience.   He loved best to see a job
finished.

Impatiently he gathered two corners of First Woman's blanket, and before she could stop him . . .

. . . he flung the remaining stars out into the night, spilling them in wild disarray, shattering First Woman's careful patterns.

First Woman leaned far into the night and watched
the tumbling stars. "What have you done, you
foolish animal!" she shrieked at Coyote. He crept
away while First Woman wept because there was
no undoing what Coyote had done.

As the pulse of the second day brought it into being,
the people rose and went about their lives, never knowing in
what foolish haste Coyote had tumbled the stars . . .

. . . never knowing the reason for the confusion that would always dwell among them.